Journey To The Top Of The Earth

by

Robert F. Robben

for my very own Petro Pals, Patrick and Elizabeth

Illustrations by Robert Jaros
Edited by Margaret Burger Robben

Copywrited in 1996
Petro Pals, Inc.
A Division of RobToy, Inc.

Library of Congress
Catalog Card Number: 96:92455

Petro Pals, Inc.
A Division of RobToy, Inc
Old Greenwich, CT

WORLD'S SUPPLY OF PETROLEUM

FULL

Once upon a time

there was

a pool of golden liquid

deep inside the center of the Earth.

The Petro Pals

lived there

with their families.

The Petro Pals sometimes imagined

what it might be like to live on

top of the Earth.

One day

the Petro Pals

heard loud noises.

They were very scared.

They went running to their

mommies and daddies.

"Don't be scared," said Daddy Crude Al.

"We must get ready to go to the top of the Earth!

The people need us in many ways."

"The sounds you heard were the people on the Earth working to make our journey safe."

The family

packed their bags

and waited their turn

to go to

the top of the Earth.

Kerry-Sene was sad

to leave

some of her friends behind.

Gaso-Lene was happy

because he would

get to see

his cousin Grease Boy again

who went to

the top of the Earth

before him.

Up Up they went!

Up went Daddy Crude Al!

Up went Mommy Light Sweet Sally!

Up went Gaso-Lene!

Up went Kerry-Sene!

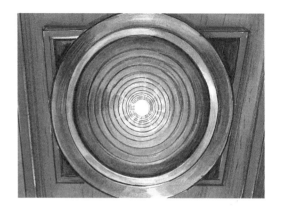

The sun was warm.

The sky was blue.

The ocean was clear.

"What a beautiful place

the top of the Earth is,"

they all said.

"There's the truck
that will bring us
to our new home!"
said Light Sweet Sally.

The truck drove past

rolling green hills,

colorful flowers

and singing birds.

"What a beautiful place

the top of the Earth is,"

they said again.

Welcome to Petropolis!

A band was playing.

Balloons were everywhere.

Grease Boy

gave his cousins,

Kerry-Sene and Gaso-Lene,

a present—

a puppy named Drip.

Everyone was happy.

Later in the day
Uncle Diesel and Aunt Ether
invited the new family
for a special meal.

They all

had many questions

to ask.

"Who is Officer Asphalt?"

asked Daddy Crude Al.

"Officer Asphalt protects the Petro Pals," said Uncle Diesel. "He knows we are all very special. He wants the people on the Earth to use us in good ways."

"What does Spillman do?"

asked Kerry-Sene.

"Spillman teaches

the people of the Earth

not to waste

and

not to spill

the

precious golden liquid,"

said Aunt Ether.

"What does Dr. Arson do?"

asked

Mommy Light Sweet Sally.

"Dr. Arson works
to make sure
the golden liquid
is not used
to start fires.
If a fire does start
his job is
to put the fire out,"
said Uncle Diesel.

"What does

Carl Catastrophe do?"

asked Gaso-Lene.

"Carl Catastrophe

safe-guards

the golden liquid

when it's being

transported by

ships, trains and trucks.

He

wants to keep

the top of the Earth

a beautiful place,"

answered Aunt Ether.

The newly arrived family

had many

of their questions

answered.

As they were

eating dessert

Grease Boy

said with excitement,

"I can't wait

until tomorrow!"

"I can't either!"

added Gaso-Lene.

"Ruff! Ruff!"

barked Drip.

He

wanted to be

in on the fun too.

To be continued....